Copyright © 1991 Award Publications Limited
This 1991 edition published by Derrydale Books,
distributed by Outlet Book Company, Inc., a Random
House Company, 225 Park Avenue South, New York,
New York 10003.

Printed and bound in Malaysia

ISBN 0-517-06524-X

87654321

Robert Louis Stevenson's

TREASURE ISLAND

Adapted by Michael Bishop

Illustrated by Gerry Embleton

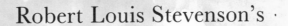

DERRYDALE BOOKS
New York

This is the story of Treasure Island as told by young Jim Hawkins after his return from his great adventure, a tale of treachery and terror.

It all began long ago on the Devonshire coast at the Admiral Benbow Inn, which was kept by Jim's parents. Jim's father was dying and being looked after by a family friend, Dr. Livesey. A weatherbeaten sailor arrived at the inn one day, complete with his old sea chest. Known as 'The Captain' he sat every evening in the parlor by the fire, drinking rum and sometimes breaking into his favorite song:

"Fifteen men on a dead man's chest
Yo-ho-ho and a bottle of rum
Drink and the devil be done with the rest
Yo-ho-ho and a bottle of rum . . ."

And every day he would wander around the cove close by the inn, or up on the cliffs overlooking the sea with his brass telescope to see what ships were passing by.

He was always suspicious of other seamen who stayed occasionally at the Admiral Benbow, and he paid Jim Hawkins a silver fourpenny to keep his 'weather-eye open for a seafaring man with one leg.' And there were hints of treasure hidden by the pirate captain, Flint.

Then one day a stranger came to the inn. The Captain turned pale when he saw him and called him 'Black Dog.' They went into the parlor together, where they talked for some time. At first their voices were kept low, but gradually they could be heard getting more and more angry.

Then a fight started and Jim saw the
Captain chasing Black Dog out of the inn,
trying to grab him and cut him down. It
was only because the Captain's cutlass
caught the inn-sign above the door that
Black Dog escaped certain death.

After this episode, the Captain was
taken ill and the doctor was sent for. Dr.
Livesey was not sympathetic. "You have
been drinking rum and you've had a
stroke," said he, and told him to stay in
bed for a week.

But before the week was up, another
visitor arrived at the inn. It was a blind
man, called Pew.

He came tap-tap-tapping with his stick
to the door, where he grabbed hold of Jim
and made him lead the way to the
Captain's room.

The blind man shoved something into
the Captain's hand—and fled.

"The Black Spot!" gasped the Captain.
But even as he saw it in his hand, the
Captain reeled over and died 'struck by a
thundering apoplexy.'

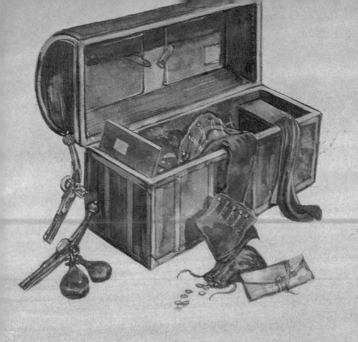

Jim guessed from these mysterious happenings that the Captain had been guarding a secret. Perhaps there was something in the old sea chest! And there were rumors in the village of a pirate lugger anchored in the cove.

He confided in his mother, who was angry because the Captain had owed them a lot of money for his lodging. Together they found a key round the dead sailor's neck. They went up to his room and opened the chest. Right at the bottom they found a bundle tied up in oilcloth and a canvas bag full of old coins.

Jim's mother would only take what was due to her, and was counting out the coins when Jim heard the tap-tapping of the blind man's stick on the road outside.

"Mother," he said urgently. "Take it all and let's be going!"

But, frightened as she was, his mother would only take as much as she had counted. Jim took the oilskin bundle and they both left the inn. As they did so they heard the sound of footsteps running towards them. They just had time to hide.

Jim saw six men and three carried a battering ram.

They were being egged on by the blind beggar, Pew. "Down with the door," he cried as they got to the inn.

"In, in, in!" he shouted as they broke down the door; and he cursed them for their delay.

Four of them went inside and found the Captain dead.

"Search him, some of you shirking lubbers," cried Pew. "And the rest of you aloft to get the chest!"

Jim could hear men running up the stairs and into the Captain's room.

"Is it there?" roared Pew.

"The money's there!"

The blind man cursed the money. "It's Flint's map we need!" he shrieked.

"We don't see it here nohow," was the reply.

"It's that boy, Hawkins!" Pew cursed. "I wish I'd put his eyes out! Scatter, lads, and find him."

The men searched the inn and looked around outside, but only half-heartedly.

"Hang it, Pew, we've got the doubloons," grumbled one of them.

"You've got your hands on thousands, you fools," shouted Pew. "You'd be as rich as kings if you could find the map!"

"They might have hid the blessed thing," said another. "Take the money, Pew, and stop squalling!"

But Pew's anger rose until his passion got the upper hand and he struck at them right and left in his blindness. They cursed back at him and threatened him in dreadful terms, trying in vain to get the stick away from him.

This quarrel saved Jim and his mother, for as the men fought there came the sound of horses galloping over the hill. The buccaneers fled leaving blind Pew to his fate.

He remained tapping up and down the road in a frenzy, groping and calling his comrades.

"You won't leave old Pew, mates, not old Pew," he pleaded.

Just then four or five riders came in sight, sweeping at full gallop towards him.

Pew tried to dodge out of the way, fell into a ditch but got to his feet again, utterly bewildered. He dashed right under the leading horse and was trampled to death.

Jim and his mother came out of hiding and hailed the riders. They turned out to be Revenue men chasing after the gang, whom they took to be smugglers.

They helped Jim and his mother back to the inn.

"What in fortune were they after?" asked Mr. Dance, their leader. "Money, I suppose?"

"No, sir, not money, I think," replied Jim. "I believe I have the thing they were after and I should like to get it put in safety."

"To be sure, boy," said Mr. Dance, "I'll take it if you like."

"I thought, perhaps, Dr. Livesey. . ." ventured Jim.

"Perfectly right," said the other cheerily.

They found Dr. Livesey at Squire Trelawney's house, and Jim was given a big pigeon pie to eat while they all talked of the oilskin bundle that Jim had found, and of the strange goings-on at the Admiral Benbow Inn.

"You've heard of this Flint, I suppose?" asked Dr. Livesey of the Squire.

"Heard of him! He was the bloodthirstiest buccaneer that sailed!"

"Supposing we have here some clue to where Flint buried his treasure—will that amount to much?" asked the Doctor.

"Amount, sir!" cried the Squire. "If we have the clue, I fit out a ship in Bristol dock and take you and Hawkins here along. I'll have that treasure if I search a year!"

And so they opened the bundle and beneath some documents they found a map.

It was the map of Treasure Island with the vital clues to find where the treasure was buried.

"Tomorrow," vowed Squire Trelawney, "I start for Bristol. We'll have the best ship, sir, and the choicest crew in England."

"Trelawney," said the Doctor, "I'll go with you and so will Jim."

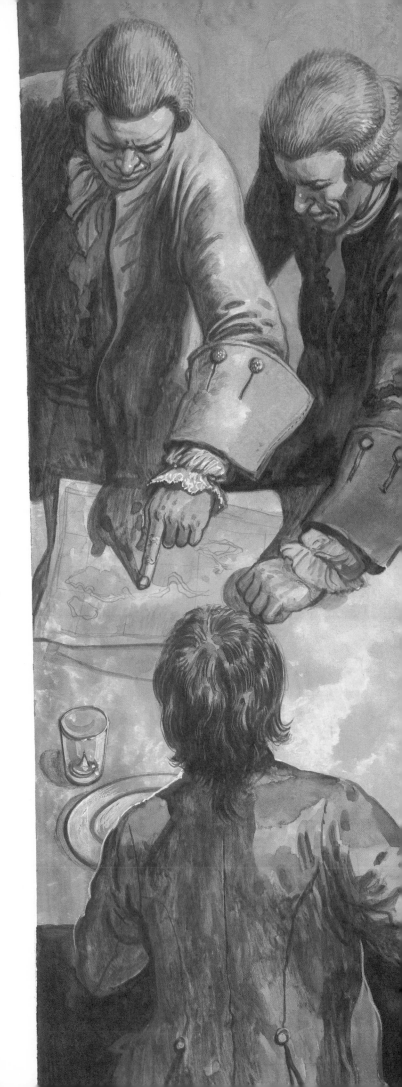

It took longer than the Squire had anticipated before there was a ship ready for sea. For safety's sake, Jim stayed at the Squire's Hall in the charge of old Redruth, the gamekeeper, full of sea-dreams and thoughts of strange islands and adventures.

At last there came a letter from the Squire saying that the ship he had bought, the Hispaniola, was fitted out and ready for sea.

He wrote that he had found a one-legged sailor called Long John Silver whom he had signed on as cook, and who had helped him find a full crew for the ship.

The Squire concluded his letter by summoning both the Doctor and Jim to Bristol post haste.

"But," he wrote, "let young Hawkins go to see his mother with my gamekeeper, Redruth, for a guard."

Jim spent the night at the Admiral Benbow Inn and the next evening he and Redruth caught the overnight mail coach to Bristol. Despite his excitement, Jim slept all the way.

It was in front of a large inn down by the docks that Squire Trelawney welcomed them. He was dressed like a sea officer in stout blue cloth and he imitated a sailor's walk.

"Here you are!" he cried. "Bravo! The ship's company complete!"

"Oh, sir!" cried Jim. "When do we sail?"

"We sail tomorrow," was the reply.

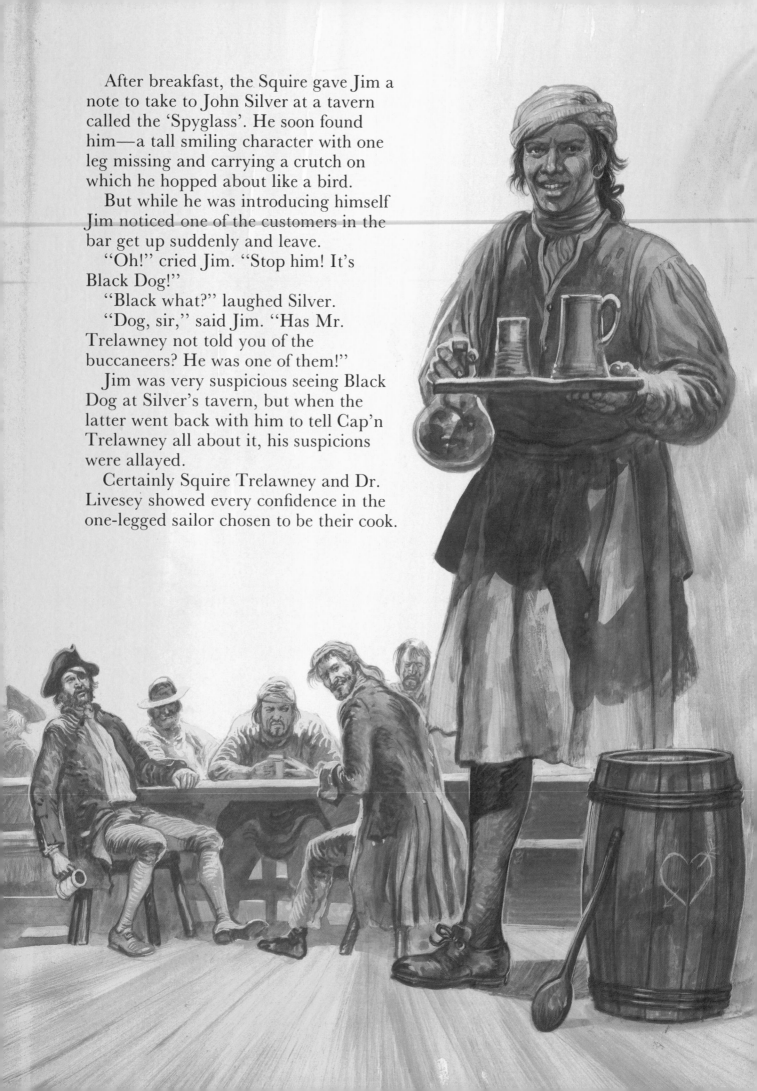

After breakfast, the Squire gave Jim a note to take to John Silver at a tavern called the 'Spyglass'. He soon found him—a tall smiling character with one leg missing and carrying a crutch on which he hopped about like a bird.

But while he was introducing himself Jim noticed one of the customers in the bar get up suddenly and leave.

"Oh!" cried Jim. "Stop him! It's Black Dog!"

"Black what?" laughed Silver.

"Dog, sir," said Jim. "Has Mr. Trelawney not told you of the buccaneers? He was one of them!"

Jim was very suspicious seeing Black Dog at Silver's tavern, but when the latter went back with him to tell Cap'n Trelawney all about it, his suspicions were allayed.

Certainly Squire Trelawney and Dr. Livesey showed every confidence in the one-legged sailor chosen to be their cook.

Not so with Captain Smollett, captain of the Hispaniola. As soon as they were on board the ship, Smollett asked to speak to the squire.

"Better speak plain, sir," he said bluntly. "I don't like this cruise. I don't like the men and I don't like my officer, Mr. Arrow. He's too familiar with the crew."

Jim could see that the Squire was furious, but Dr. Livesey pacified him. Captain Smollett went on: "I find that every man before the mast knows we're going after treasure," and he advised that all the arms and gunpowder, at that moment being stored near the crew's quarters, should be stored instead under the officers' cabin. This was quickly agreed.

"And the crew know that you have a map of an island with crosses to show where the treasure is," continued Captain Smollett. "I don't know who has this map, but I want it kept secret from me and Mr. Arrow."

"You wish to keep this matter dark," said the Doctor, "and to make a garrison

of the stern part of the ship. In other words, you fear a mutiny?"

"Sir, I ask you to take certain precautions."

The Squire was still angry, but Captain Smollett had made his point. With that, they all went up on deck again to see the crew at work.

The men were already hard at it taking out the arms and powder to stow them aft, yo-ho-hoing at their work. The last man or two came on board from a shore boat. With them was Long John Silver.

He came up the side like a monkey and as soon as he saw what was happening, "So, ho, mates," says he. "What's doing?"

"My orders!" barked the Captain. "You may go below and cook the supper."

"Ay, ay, sir," answered the cook, and, touching his forelock, he disappeared at once in the direction of the galley.

"That's a good man, Captain," said the Doctor.

"Very likely, sir," replied Captain Smollett.

Just then the Captain saw Jim Hawkins idling amidships, watching all the activity. "Here, you, ship's boy!" he cried. "Off with you to the cook and get some work!"

"I'll have no favourites on my ship," he said loudly to the Doctor.

All that night there was a great bustle getting things stowed in their right place and ready for sea. Boatsful of the Squire's friends came out to wish him a good voyage and a safe return.

Jim Hawkins was dog-tired when, a little before dawn, the boatswain sounded his pipe and the crew manned the capstan to raise the ship's anchor. And, led by Long John Silver, they began to chant the ditty that Jim knew so well:

> "Fifteen men on a dead man's chest
> Yo-ho-ho and a bottle of rum . . ."

Soon the anchor was up, the sails were hoisted and began to catch the wind. And before the sun was up, the Hispaniola was at sea, dipping her bows into the waves, and beginning her long voyage to Treasure Island.

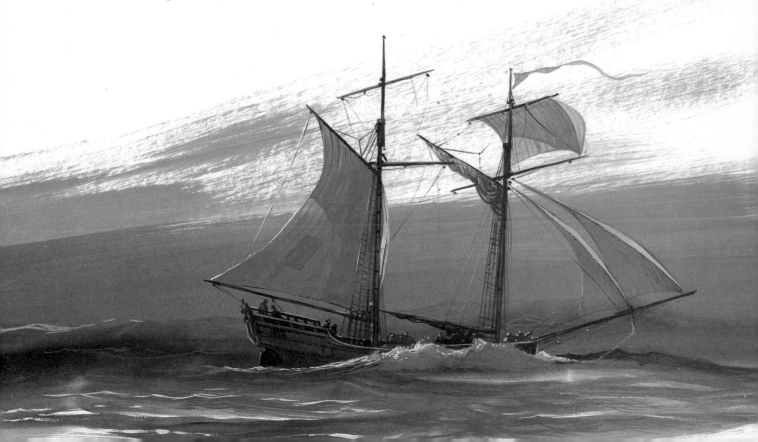

Early in the voyage, Mr. Arrow the mate, turned out to be an even worse officer than the Captain had feared. He was not only a bad influence among the men, but he was often drunk. Then one dark night he disappeared overboard and was never seen again.

Job Anderson, the boatswain, took the place of the lost mate, helped by Israel Hands, the Coxswain, a wily and experienced seaman who was a great confidant of Long John Silver.

Jim spent much time in the ship's galley where he met Long John's parrot.

"I calls my parrot Cap'n Flint after the famous buccaneer," Long John told him.

And the parrot would say "Pieces of eight! Pieces of eight!" till you wondered that it was not out of breath.

Captain Smollet, for his part, was still on bad terms with the Squire but he upheld strict discipline over the crew.

And so they sailed across the ocean for many weeks and it was during the last evening of the outward voyage—with most of the crew forward in the bows looking out for the island—when Jim fancied an apple from the barrel kept on deck. By then, the barrel was almost empty and he hopped inside.

No sooner had he sat down in the barrel to chew an apple when a heavy man sat down close by and leaned against it. Jim was about to jump up when he heard Silver's voice—and what he heard kept him sitting there, trembling with fear.

For Long John was talking to some of the crew, telling them of some of his experiences and of his plans. He had been quartermaster on board the old 'Walrus,' Captain Flint's ship, and he revealed that many of Flint's men were now on board the 'Hispaniola.' At the right time they were going to take over the ship.

It was the voice of the coxswain, Israel Hands, who growled, "How long are we a-going to stand off and on like a blessed bum-boat? I've had almost enough of Captain Smollett!"

"Till I give the word," cried Silver. "The last moment I can manage. This Squire and the Doctor have a map—they shall find the stuff and help us get it aboard. Then we'll see!"

"Only one thing I claim," he went on. "I claim Trelawney—I'll wring his neck with these hands."

Then he asked one of the men to jump up and get him an apple from the barrel. Jim was terrified—but he was saved by Israel Hands, who suggested having some rum instead.

Jim could hear them drinking. "Here's to old Flint!" said one; and Silver himself was saying, "Here's to ourselves and hold your luff, plenty of prizes and plenty of duff!"

Just then a sort of brightness fell on Jim in the barrel and he found that the moon had risen and was shining white on the sails.

And almost at the same time the voice of one of the look-outs was heard shouting, "Land-ho!"

There was a rush of feet across the deck—and Jim slipped quickly out of the barrel. He joined the rest of the crew in the bows to get his first glimpse of Treasure Island.

And as soon as he could get close enough to the Doctor without being overheard, he said, "Doctor, get the Captain and the Squire down to the cabin. I have terrible news!"

Captain Smollett spoke to the crew, told them that they had reached their destination and that grog would be served to celebrate. And while the men were thus happily engaged, a council of war was held in the cabin.

Jim Hawkins recounted all that he had heard in the apple barrel. When he had finished they gave him a glass of wine and they all drank his health for his luck and his courage.

"We must go on," said Captain Smollett, "because we can't turn back. We have time on our side, at least until the treasure's found. And we've got some faithful hands."

But when they counted heads, there were only seven of the twenty-six on board on whom they could rely. And one of the seven was a boy—Jim Hawkins.

As soon as the Hispaniola was anchored in a safe haven (pointed out by Long John Silver himself) the conduct of the crew became alarming. They lay about the deck, growling in talk. So it was decided in the cabin to hand out loaded pistols to all the loyal hands.

Captain Smollett then went up on deck and told the men that as many as wanted could go ashore in one of the boats.

Jim Hawkins slipped unseen into the first boat away.

And the moment the boat struck the shore, Jim was out and running into the nearest thicket.

Although he was still scared, Jim began to enjoy exploring this strange land; he saw flowering plants he had never seen before, and a snake hissed at him.

Then he heard voices in the distance. One he recognized as Long John Silver's. Jim crept closer.

Long John was trying to persuade one of the crew called Tom to join the rebels—when they suddenly heard a sound like a cry of anger, followed by one horrid, long-drawn out scream that echoed across the island.

"In heaven's name, what was that?" gasped Tom.

"Oh, I reckon that'll be Alan," said Silver with a wicked grin.

"You've killed Alan?" cried Tom. "Kill me too, if you can. But I defies you!"

And with that the brave fellow turned his back on Silver and walked away. Long John whipped the crutch out of his armpit and hurled it at Tom's back, knocking him down.

Agile as a monkey, with knife in hand, Silver was on top of him in a moment—and he stabbed him twice in the back.

Jim almost fainted at the sight. "They've killed Alan and Tom. Will I be the next?" he wondered.

But he quickly pulled himself together and ran as fast as he could from the scene—till a fresh alarm made him stop with his heart thumping.

He had seen a man-like creature dodging between the trees. After much hesitation he came out to meet Jim.

"Who are you?" asked Jim.

"I'm poor Ben Gunn," was the reply. "Marooned here three years ago and lived on goats and berries ever since."

Jim learned from him that he had been on board Flint's ship when the treasure had been buried. Later, in another ship, the crew had come ashore on this island to search for the treasure. But in their frustration at not being able to find it, they had marooned Ben Gunn!

He promised to help Jim in return for a passage back to England in the Hispaniola. Ben was just telling Jim about the small boat he had built when they heard the sound of gunfire and Jim saw, in the distance over some woods, the Union Jack fluttering in the air.

Still on board the Hispaniola, the Squire, the Doctor and the Captain had been worried about Jim and alarmed for his safety. It was decided that the Doctor and one of the loyal seamen, Hunter, should go ashore to look at the stockade marked on the chart.

They had found it an ideal place to hold out against the rebels, so the others had followed them ashore.

They soon heard voices of the buccaneers close by and it became a race as to which party would get to the stockade first. Both got to the clearing at the same time.

The Squire and the Doctor were able to fire shots at the seven mutineers. One of them was killed and the rest fled into the trees—but not before firing a shot which killed the faithful Redruth.

As soon as they were safely inside the stockade, Captain Smollett hoisted the British flag—the fluttering flag that Jim and Ben Gunn had seen in the distance.

As evening fell, two of the loyal seamen volunteered to go back to their boat to rescue some of the stores of food. They were unlucky. The mutineers had got there first.

But it wasn't all bad news! A little later, safe and sound, Jim Hawkins came climbing over the stockade.

Jim quickly told of his adventures and of his meeting with Ben Gunn. Then Captain Smollett organized his small garrison in the stockade into two watches—it was feared that they would be starved into surrender because they had so little food.

But Jim Hawkins was dog-tired and despite all the dangers around him, he slept like a log.

He was awakened by the sound of voices. "Flag of truce!" he heard. "Silver himself!"

"Well?" demanded Captain Smollett.

"We want that treasure," said Silver, "and we'll have it!"

"That's as maybe," said the Captain.

"You give us the chart to get the treasure by," continued Silver.

"Come aboard along of us once the treasure's shipped and I'll give you my word of honor to clap you somewhere safe ashore. Or else you can stay here and we'll divide stores with you man for man."

"Now you'll hear me," answered Captain Smollett. "Come in one by one, and I'll clap you all in irons and take you home to a fair trial in England. If you don't, I'll see you all to Davy Jones!"

Silver's face was a picture; his eyes started in his head with wrath. "Before the hour's out," he cried, "I'll attack your old blockhouse! Them that die will be the lucky ones!"

And with a dreadful oath, he stumbled off.

The attack when it came was sudden enough. There was a brief exchange of musket shots, then, with a loud 'Huzza!', a little crowd of pirates leapt from the woods and ran for the stockade. They swarmed over the fence like monkeys; two were hit and one fled but several got inside and in a moment were upon the defenders in the loghouse.

"Out, lads, and fight 'em in the open!" cried the Captain in the midst of the smoke and confusion.

This tactic won the day and very soon three of the attackers were down and a fourth was clambering out of the stockade with the fear of death upon him. In no time the others were fleeing with him back to the woods.

So they fought off the first attack.

But, back in the loghouse, they saw the price they had paid for victory. Hunter lay stunned; Joyce had been shot through the head; and the Squire was supporting Captain Smollett.

"The Captain's wounded," said Mr. Trelawney.

"Have they run?" asked the Captain.

"All that could," answered the Doctor. "But there's five of them will never run again!"

"Five!" exclaimed the Captain. "Five against three—that leaves four of us to nine of them. Better odds than when we started!"

The Captain's injuries were serious but not fatal. The Doctor patched him up and then, a little while later, put the chart in his pocket, armed himself, and walked out of the stockade into the trees.

Jim was surprised at the Doctor's departure, but then guessed that he had gone off to see Ben Gunn. This put an idea into Jim's head.

While the others weren't looking he stuffed his pockets full of biscuits, grabbed a brace of pistols and found some powder and bullets.

He had made up his mind to see if he could find the place where Ben Gunn had hidden his boat.

The Squire and Gray were busy helping the Captain with his bandages and Jim made a bolt for it, over the stockade and into the thickest of the trees.

He made his way down to the beach, from where he could see the Hispaniola— with the Jolly Roger flying from her masthead.

Jim found Ben Gunn's boat. It was very small, even for Jim, and was made of wood and goatskin.

"The worst coracle ever made," thought Jim. But the idea was forming in his mind to cut the Hispaniola adrift in order to foil any plans the buccaneers might have to sail away.

He launched the coracle and with the aid of a paddle he made his way out to the ship. He grabbed the hawser, took his knife from his pocket, opened it with his teeth and waited for the hawser to slacken off.

As a gust of wind caught the ship, he sliced through the rope. He had set the Hispaniola adrift!

That was the beginning of Jim's perilous voyage in the coracle. Both the Hispaniola and the tiny craft drifted out to sea on the ebb tide, but Jim found that he was quite unable to control his boat. In constant danger of capsizing, he lay down in the bottom and (so exhausted was he) went to sleep!

It was broad daylight when he awoke and found himself tossed about in a rough sea some way off the coast of Treasure Island. He tried paddling but this produced such violent changes in the behavior of the coracle that he had to give up.

He was drenched and horribly frightened, but kept his head.

As he got used to the movement of the boat he was able to judge when he could use the paddle to give her a shove or two towards the land.

It was slow and tiring work. He began to be tortured by thirst. He was getting quite close to the land, but the current took him past the headland he was aiming for. And then, beyond the headland, he suddenly saw the Hispaniola again!

The ship was under sail, but behaving very erratically. Nevertheless, they were coming closer together all the time.

Jim felt sure that he would be captured if he got on board, but his thirst was so great he did not really care.

So, as the coracle came underneath the bowsprit of the Hispaniola, on the crest of a wave, Jim leapt up and grabbed hold of the rope beneath the jib boom. He hauled himself up and on board the ship.

Jim soon found the two buccaneers who had been left on board. One of them was spreadeagled on the deck, dead. The other was Israel Hands, lying nearby propped up against the bulwarks, nearly dead. There had obviously been a fight, with bloodstains on the planks.

When he rolled over and saw Jim there, all that Israel Hands could say was: "Brandy!" Jim got himself a drink of water first, and some biscuits to eat before giving the coxswain what he wanted. "By thunder!" said he. "But I needed some of that!"

"I've come aboard to take possession of the ship," announced Jim, and he took down the skull and crossbones flag.

Hands could see that he was helpless and he struck a bargain with Jim. "You give me food and drink and an old scarf to tie my wound up and I'll tell you how to sail the ship and put her safely on the beach." Jim agreed, helped him bandage his wound and gave him some food.

Then he took the tiller and under the coxswain's instructions, he took the Hispaniola round the northern end of Treasure island, safely into the North Inlet. He was struggling with the tiller to bring the ship safely to the shore, when he sensed trouble behind him.

And there was Israel Hands coming at him with a dagger in his hand.

As their eyes met, Hands threw himself forward with a roar of fury. Jim leapt sideways and let go of the tiller. The tiller swung back and struck Hands across the chest, stopping him dead.

Before he could recover from the blow, Jim got away from the corner where he'd been trapped and out on to the open deck. He stopped by the mainmast, took a pistol from his pocket and took careful aim. Hands was already coming after him again.

Jim pulled the trigger—but nothing happened. The powder was damp and useless. Realizing that it would be a waste of time trying to use the other pistol, he hastily dodged behind the mast.

Wounded though he was, Hands had been moving fast. But now he paused, wondering which way Jim would go.

Suddenly the Hispaniola struck the shore and canted over. Both Jim and Hands were taken by surprise and they fell in a heap in the scuppers.

Jim was first to recover. He scrambled up quickly and sprang into the shrouds to climb up to the cross-trees halfway up the mast.

Hands stabbed at him as he went and only missed by inches.

Safe for the moment, sitting on the crosstrees, Jim hastily reprimed his pistols with fresh powder. Hands saw what was happening and began slowly and painfully to climb up the shrouds after Jim, his knife in his teeth.

But with his wounds it took him a long time and Jim had his pistols reloaded before he was more than a third of the way up.

With a pistol in either hand, Jim called out, "One more step, Mr. Hands, and I'll blow your brains out."

He stopped instantly and Jim could see by the look of his face that he was trying to figure out what to do next. He took the dagger from his mouth in order to speak.

"I reckon we're fouled, Jim, you and me, and we'll have to sign articles . . ."

Even as he spoke, Hands threw his knife. It sang like an arrow through the air and Jim felt a blow and then a sharp pang—and he was pinned by the shoulder to the mast.

In the pain and surprise of the moment—he said afterwards that he never took aim—both his pistols went off and they both fell out of his hands.

They did not fall alone; with a choked cry, the coxswain lost his grip and plunged headfirst into the shallow sea.

The body rose to the surface once, then sank again for good.

Jim found that the knife thrown by Hands had only pinched his skin and he was able to release himself quickly.

He tipped the body of the second mutineer overboard and he set about making the ship as safe as he could. She was firmly beached and he lowered those sails that he could manage, cutting the ropes where necessary.

Satisfied that he had done all he could, he scrambled up into the bows of the ship. The sun was now setting and it was getting chilly. Taking hold of the end of the hawser that he had cut earlier to set the ship adrift, he went down hand over hand into the water, which, he was relieved to find, only came up to his waist.

He waded ashore, nursing his wounded arm but in good spirits.

"There lies the schooner," he said to himself, "clear at last from buccaneers and ready for our own men to get to sea again." He might be blamed for his 'truantry' but he hoped that even Captain Smollet would be pleased with the re-capture of the Hispaniola.

And so he set off through the woods again to find his friends in the stockade. Gradually the night got blacker; the landmarks he had been following to find his way got fainter: the stars were few and pale and he kept tripping over bushes and rolling into sandy pits. Then, suddenly a kind of brightness fell about him and a silvery light filtered through the trees. A full moon was rising to guide him on his way.

As he got close to the stockade he went very warily. He was surprised to see the glowing embers left from an immense fire close to the blockhouse—the Captain's orders had been not to use too much firewood.

The last few yards to the house he crawled on hands and knees. He cheered up a bit when he heard snoring from within. As he reached the door, he stood up and felt his way into the darkness inside. He stumbled over a sleeper's leg.

And then, all of a sudden, a shrill voice woke everybody: "Pieces of eight! Pieces of eight! Pieces of eight!"

It was Silver's parrot, Captain Flint.

"Bring a torch," said the voice of Long John Silver. "Let's see who goes!"

And when the light arrived: "Jim Hawkins, shiver my timbers! Dropped in, like, eh?"

And so began Jim's day as a hostage in the enemy's camp. Silver told him that Dr. Livesey had been down to see the buccaneers with a flag of truce. He had told them that the Hispaniola had gone and offered to bargain.

"So here we are," said Silver. "Stores, brandy, chart. As for them, I don't know where they are."

But Long John did not have it all his own way. The rest of the pirates put the black spot on him and told him that he was deposed as their leader. Silver's reply was to produce the chart showing where the treasure was hidden. This soon put a stop to their rebellion.

And when the Doctor came next day to see to the wounded ones, Silver allowed Jim to talk to him through the stockade fence.

The Doctor tried to persuade Jim to cut and run, but Jim wouldn't—he had given his word of honor to Long John Silver. However, he told the Doctor where he had left the Hispaniola.

"The ship!" exclaimed the Doctor.

Quickly Jim described to him his adventures.

"There's a kind of fate in this," said the Doctor in wonderment. "Every step, it's you that saves our lives, Jim! Silver!" he cried, "Silver, I'll give you a piece of advice—look out for squalls if you find the treasure!"

And with that, Doctor Livesey shook hands with Jim through the stockade fence, nodded to Silver, and set off at a brisk pace into the wood.

After a hearty breakfast cooked by the now confident buccaneers, Silver tied a rope round Jim's waist and led him off to search for the treasure. The other men carried picks and shovels for digging and enough food for a midday meal.

As they approached the area where, according to the map, the treasure was buried, they spread out. Suddenly, out of the trees, a high trembling voice was heard:-

"Fifteen men on a dead man's chest
Yo-ho-ho and a bottle of rum . . ."

The buccaneers were terrified. The color went from their faces like magic. Silver tried to rally them—but again the same voice was heard:-

"Darby McGraw! Fetch aft the rum, Darby!"

"They was Flint's last words," gasped one of the pirates. "Let's go!" cried another.

But Silver was not to be beaten. "I'm here to get that treasure and I'll not be beat by man nor devil," he muttered.

"True it was not Flint's voice," admitted one of the men, "it was more like somebody else's voice—more like . . ."

"By the powers, Ben Gunn!" roared Long John Silver.

"Aye, Ben Gunn it were! Nobody minds Ben Gunn, dead or alive."

Much relieved, their spirits revived and the natural color returned to their faces. Soon they shouldered their tools and set off again. The thought of seven hundred thousand pounds in gold buried just ahead of them made them forget their terrors.

Silver hobbled, grunting, on his crutch. He plucked furiously at the line that held Jim to him and, from time to time, turned his eyes on Jim with a deadly look.

Jim was sure that he hoped to seize the treasure, find the Hispaniola again and cut every honest throat on the island. Then to sail away as he had first intended, laden with crimes and riches.

But when they got to the spot where the treasure should have been buried, all they found was a hole in the ground

and the remains of several packing cases—one piece of wood branded with the word 'Wulrus'—the name of Flint's ship.

The treasure was gone!

Long John Silver kept his head and changed his plan before the others had time to realize their disappointment. He passed a double-barreled pistol to Jim "Take that," he whispered, "and stand by for trouble."

At the same time he was edging round the hollow in the ground away from the rest of the men.

They dug furiously with their fingers in the dusty earth and sand. One of them found a two-guinea gold piece.

"Two guineas!" he roared at Silver. "That's your seven hundred thousand pounds, is it?"

They all scrambled out of the excavation on the opposite side to Jim and Silver.

"Mates," said one, "there's two of them alone there. One's the old cripple with one leg, the other's that cub I mean to have the heart of . . ."

Cutlass in hand, he raised his arm
to lead a charge . . . But just then
crack! crack! crack! three musket shots
flashed out of the thicket. Two of the
men were killed, the others ran for
their lives.

The Doctor, Gray and Ben Gunn
appeared from the trees with muskets
still smoking.

"Thank you kindly, Doctor," said
Silver. "You came in the nick of time
for me and young Hawkins here. And
Ben Gunn! You're a nice one, to be
sure!"

"How do, Mr. Silver?" replied the
maroon, wriggling with
embarrassment.

"Ben," muttered Long John, "to
think as you've done me!"

On the way back to find the Squire and the wounded Captain Smollett, Jim and Silver heard Ben Gunn's story.

In his lone wanderings about the island after being marooned, he had found the treasure. He had dug it up and had carried it on his back in many weary journeys to a cave he had discovered in another part of the island.

When the Doctor had wormed this secret out of him, he had gone to Silver and had given him the chart which was now useless. He had also given him the stores of food, because Ben Gunn's cave was well supplied. He would have given him anything to get a chance of moving in safety from the stockade to keep guard on the treasure cave.

That morning, when he had found out that Jim had been taken hostage, and was going to be involved in their search for the treasure, the Doctor had run all the way back to the cave to fetch Gray and Ben Gunn.

They had set off to try to be where the treasure had been buried before the buccaneers. But the latter were ahead of them. So Ben Gunn had been sent ahead to do his best alone—and he had been so successful that Gray and the Doctor had already been in ambush before the arrival of the treasure hunters.

"It were fortunate for me that I had Hawkins here," said Long John Silver. "You would have let old John be cut to bits and never given it a thought."

"Not a thought," replied the Doctor cheerily.

And so they came to the cave, where the Squire met them. To Jim he was cordial and kind, saying nothing of his escapade. In reply to Silver's polite salute he said: "John Silver, you're a prodigious villain!"

"Thank you kindly, sir," said Long John, saluting again.

Jim saw great heaps of coins and bars of gold—Flint's treasure that they had come so far to seek and that had cost the lives of seventeen men from the Hispaniola.

"Come in, Jim," said Captain Smollett from where he lay beside a fire. "You're a good boy—but I don't think you or me'll go to sea again."

What a supper they had that night! Ben Gunn's salted goat and other delicacies and a bottle of old wine from the Hispaniola. And there was Long John Silver, the same helpful, polite seaman of the voyage out.

It took them the best part of three days to load the treasure on to the Hispaniola. All the time, they had to guard against attack from the surviving buccaneers. However they heard nothing but some drunken singing.

As soon as they could, they weighed anchor and the Hispaniola sailed away from Treasure Island. Being so short of men, they headed for the nearest port in Spanish America to pick up a crew.

The Doctor, the Squire and Jim went ashore as night was falling—and they had such an agreeable time that it was daybreak before they got back to the ship. Ben Gunn met them and confessed that he had helped Long John Silver to get away in a shore boat. And he had not gone empty handed—he had cut through a bulkhead unobserved and had removed one of the sacks of coins worth about three or four hundred pounds.

In fact, they were all pleased to get rid of him so cheaply!

With some extra hands on board, they had a good cruise back to Bristol. And all of them had an ample share of the treasure. Captain Smollett retired from the sea; Ben Gunn got a thousand pounds, which he spent (or lost) in three weeks.

And Jim Hawkins? "Nothing would drag me back to that accursed island," he said. "The worst dreams I ever have are when I hear the sharp voice of Captain Flint, the parrot, still ringing in my ears—'Pieces of eight! Pieces of eight!'"

Given by J. Flint to Mr Bones master of ye
Walrus Wlnt